A beautiful story of loss, told in a way that surprises you. The moments are captured with subtle storytelling, and the heart shines with all the small things between them. These stories hold sharp dialogue and sometimes uncomfortable encounters; these feel like real people building real relationships. Friendship and love resonate in these pages, and the ending is both surprising and perfect. And Kit, Kit Kit, is at the centre of it all. Exceptional storytelling!
~ Michelle Elvy, Bath Novella-in-Flash Award Judge 2021

Published by Ad Hoc Fiction.
www.AdHocFiction.com



Purchasing Information:
Paperback available from www.AdHocFiction.com
E-book available from all usual outlets.

Printed in the United Kingdom.
First Printing 2021.

ISBN paperback 978-1-912095-41-4
ISBN e-Book 978-1-912095-40-7

# Small Things

*by*

Hannah Sutherland

AdHoc Fiction

*To my boys, T & R*

# Contents

# When gobshite Paddy drinks, the whole town knows it

Jude MacAlennan laughs and his reflection laughs right back, the double of his Da.

Sure, it's the same face he's had his entire life, but tonight, on his legal birthday, his face looks different. Everything's larger, more animated than before: pupils, eyes, smile.

He's grinning, washing his hands, lathering on vanilla soap which soothes him when he looks up. Gasps. Catches the scribbled insult, big bold letters on the cubicle wall of the pub toilet he's never been in before. Sure, there's plenty of Paddies in town, but there's only one Paddy MacAlennan, publicly shamed.

He hears his colleagues say, 'Jude, feckin hurry up, take a piss, come and down more shots, birthday boy.' And so he shouts, 'Aye, sure, give me a min,' tries to cover the quaver in his voice.

A shiver climbs up Jude's vertebrae as he reads the scrawl again; his face pales before him in the mirror until he's practically translucent. It feels like someone's turned off the colour in a black-and-white movie without warning.

And then he's in the cubicle, below the scribbled lies, vomiting bile, and soon he'll join his friends, newly composed, and he'll laugh raucously like he's without a care in the world, down those acidic shots and dance and forget. He'll reluctantly kiss Una who wants to fuck him, shaking his head, saying, 'Nah not tonight, another night, maybe,' and it's not until he's home in his tiny flat with icicles forming in the corners of the windows like unsolicited spiderwebs, his Da passed out on the sofa, mouth catching flies, empty bottle in one hand, an undignified shadow covering his crotch, that he'll remember the sting.

He'll shake the words from the cubicle away.

He'll barely believe this is the same Da who tickled his tummy to make him giggle when he was younger, who used to cook three-course dinners in which they'd gorge themselves with turkey and stuffing until they were fit to burst and then sit by the fireplace watching the flames curl around the logs, tummies and hearts full.

He'll drape the tartan blanket over his snoring Da and as he does this, he'll remember how lovely this very fabric felt on his juvenile skin as his Da tucked him in when he was very little. He'll see his late Mammy's face light up like moonrise watching her boys, feeling happier than she does most days. He'll feel their roots woven and entwined, forever connected. He'll inhale the blanket greedily, sniffing hints of lavender and vanilla, which always soothe and make him sleep deeply.

And as he watches his Da's chest fall and rise, his face looking more innocent and relaxed than it's been in ages, the smells and comforts of his childhood and Mammy gone but imprinted fiercely in his memories, Jude will wonder if growing up means something more profound than drinking and fucking and freedom after all. He'll look at the inviting empty armchair next to the sofa and think how lonely it looks.

'Ah, Da,' he'll whisper softly, sadly, barely audible, kissing Paddy's forehead, 'I've got you. Let's get you cleaned up.'

# Growing up and old

Get a boyfriend, husband. Tick tick, tickety tick. Winning at life and you're only seventeen. Practically drooling you're so smug.

There's the other girls at school saying, 'Sure, she's tied herself down too young, thrown away her entire life before it's even begun,' but when looker Paddy MacAlennan in the year above is sweet on ye, *the* Paddy MacAlennan, ye don't wait for some better lad to come along because, sure as hell, there's no better lad in the whole town than him, the country, the world, ye reckon. When you're seventeen.

He charms with cheap bottles of wine in the local park, behind the bike sheds, tucks fallen locks of hair behind your ears, whispers into your neck, kisses ye there too until ye feel sexy, brilliant, say, 'Oh that feels brilliant Paddy,' just so he knows too. Show him your leg, just lift up your skirt so he can see it. Smile when he tells ye you're beautiful. Believe it for a wee while. Let him suck on ye until your neck's red raw and you've to cover the bites with a fancy new hairstyle and silky scarf that slips off anyway and everyone knows and calls ye a slut behind your back, to your face, to your brother Ted who breaks their noses. 'They deserve it, talking about ye like that Madeline,' Ted says proudly, blowing on his bleeding knuckles, as though violence solves words.

Continue to court Paddy. The parks. The harbour. Fuck in the dark. Associate him with the smell of sap in your nostrils, the noise of cars whizzing past, the fear of being caught, the excitement of your boldness.

Let Paddy slip his hand up your skirt. The waves lap to your left, the gulls squawk to your right, sea air blows your hair and so you feel like a movie star. Say yes when he asks ye to marry him with his fingers inside ye, as if ye could say no to that.

The wedding's small. Neither of ye have jobs and so it's up to your parents to pay and they're all broke but they can put on a good afterparty in the backie and sure, that's what a wedding's all about; the party.

Wear a white dress. Feel pretty. Smile for the photographs. Try to act like you're still a virgin. Hold the bouquet over your wee bump. Pretend you've the hiccups instead of jumping with every tiny baby kick. Feel devious and grown-up and brilliant. Revel in your secrecy. Give Paddy knowing glances only the two of ye understand. Christ, how ye love him. How he loves you.

Be supportive when Paddy starts working long hours at the harbour and you're left behind, bored senseless, growing, expanding, making room in your body and home. Be supportive when he likes a drink with the lads after working those long, long hours, physical hours, weather-beaten hours, sure, it's only one, where's the harm in that? He's still young, so young, so immature, so naïve. Ye both are.

Hide your sorrow when your first baby is born silent, the one from the wedding. Bury them. Cry lots and lots until your eyes are red raw and you've aged a decade. Ye wonder if your wee sleeping baby saw what they were letting themselves in for with the pair of ye, still children yourselves, decided no thanks. 'Don't be so feckin stupid. What a terrible thing to say,' Mammy tells ye, slaps your cheeks until they burn. 'Christ, you're a nasty wee girl so ye are, Madeline,' and so ye don't tell her how you're feeling ever again. Ye swallow your thoughts. Silly me, ye think, silly, silly, little me.

There's another baby. And another. They aren't with ye for so long as the first. Ye don't tell anyone about them except Paddy who strokes your cheek and tells ye it will all be okay. One day. Ye don't name them, not out loud. Hurts too much.

And then comes Jude. Jude with his rosebud lips and button nose, his long, long lashes and angelic infant face. Jude who coos and gurgles, and sleeps all day and wakes all night, who feeds from ye and depends on ye and loves ye. He's so tiny you're terrified ye'll break him, tiny bones, weak bones, baby bones. He's the most beautiful thing you've ever seen and although you're biased, because let's face it, every Mammy is with their own, he really is remarkable.

Ye imagine his bright future in your head before you've even left the hospital. He'll run and skin his knees playing with his friends, be a swimmer, or a musician, do well at school because he'll be clever with his magnificent brain in a way that you and Paddy never were, be a swot, stick in, soak it up, an eager sponge. You'll encourage it all. He'll go to college, get a good job, a proper money job, and buy a house of his own and look after ye and Paddy and his wife and kids, and he'll have it all and you'll be so proud. He'll fill the void in your life ye feel ye need filling to feel whole again. And when he looks up at ye beneath the wool blankets your Mammy's been knitting for all these years, hoping, praying ye get to keep just one, just one wee baby to love, ye think you're the happiest girl in the world.

Jude is enough.

# The character assassination

Mammy's in a foul mood.

Da's working at the shipyard, operating the cranes, taking on extra shifts because he says they really need the money and although they really do, Mammy's furious with him. She's feeling self-conscious and vulnerable – Jude, twelve, knows this is because she's changed her outfit seven times in forty-two minutes and she's still unhappy with what she's wearing even though Jude thinks she looks lovely – and she's snapping at them both, at the door handle when it foolishly catches the sleeve of her jacket and yanks her backwards, at the gravel that creeps into her boots and rubs her ankles as they pound the pavements on the walk to school, at the car which decides to turn right without indicating just as they step on the road to cross; she's livid with them all.

She has to attend parents' night herself, you see, without Da, and she really doesn't want to do this. Jude overhears her telling his Da that the other mammies look down their noses at her, say nasty things behind her back; she's too common, too ordinary, too loud.

Jude wants to tell her none of that matters. Their kids are all arseholes anyway and when he finishes school, he won't see them so she shouldn't stress. They matter very little to him. Besides, he's got Kit so why would he need anyone else?

When they arrive at school, they're greeted with sly side-eyes and smirks; Mammy isn't wearing designer clothing, her hair isn't perfect, her skin's problematic. Mammy raises her chin and puts on a façade of confidence, seemingly unbothered, which Jude knows will tire her to bed for the next few days, and he wants to tell her to just drop the act and relax, it doesn't matter, it really doesn't matter, but he doesn't.

She's tugging at her shirt collar as a blush spreads up her neck, says, 'Christ, it's feckin roasting in here. Is it feckin roasting in here Jude or is it just me?'

Jude tells her, 'Aye, it is,' and then he pushes his hands deep in his pockets as though by doing this, he is removing his body from this very evening.

The English teacher tells Mammy Jude's incredibly quiet, doesn't join in with the class discussions, looks like he's daydreaming half the time, doodles in his jotter, disengaged. Uninterested. Aloof. Doesn't speak to the others in his year at all. It's a worry.

'Is that so, Jude?' Mammy looks at him, her mouth a thin line, eyes dark and flat. Her body shakes with every negative word said about Jude, as though it's a personal insult against herself which physically hurts.

He shrugs, says, 'I'm just selective.'

It's the same story in Maths and History and by this point Mammy's extremely agitated, keeps saying he needs to make more of an effort, oh, how he doesn't want the reputation of being weird. Not at the tender age of twelve, goodness.

'I'm not weird, Mammy.'

And then she grabs his hand and pulls him towards the Art department, holding it so hard he thinks it may crumble into dust if she holds it for a moment longer, until he says, 'Ouch, that really hurts.' He's pulling himself away from her grip when they turn the corner, and he sees Kit. Only Kit looks sad and his face doesn't wear his beaming smile that Jude loves. The smile that stops Jude in his tracks, makes the rest of the world disappear and fade until he's the only one who exists.

And so he looks, curiously, as Kit's Da pushes his back, cursing him, saying he's an embarrassment, and Kit's looking down and his face is flushed as though he's hating every moment. And Jude wants nothing more than to run over to Kit and cheer him up but something stops him and so he remains, pausing, outside the Art department with his Mammy complaining of the heat, tugging at her collar again.

Mammy cheers up after speaking to Mr Watts, Jude's Art teacher, who lavishes praise on Jude so much it embarrasses him, says, 'Oh, he's so very talented, our Jude MacAlennan. We've a wee superstar on our hands here.' And Mammy's face brightens and she's smiling widely and nodding, absorbing everything he's saying, and she suddenly forgets she's too hot and is instead just incredibly proud. 'That's my boy,' she is saying. 'That's my boy.'

It's the over-the-top compliments and the incredible encouragement and the gushing which Jude finds a bit too much. He flushes even more than when his character was being assassinated by teachers who teach subjects he couldn't give a fuck about.

But hey, at least Mammy's happy.

# Jude doesn't understand the fascination with the pub. Not one bit

Jude's eighteen, in the pub, sitting with Una pressed up against him. She's two years older than him and has newly moved to the area. She's stroking his knee. He glances down at it now and again; he doesn't dislike the gesture, just finds the touching under the table odd. Different.

They're sitting with a group of his colleagues and he's sipping a pint, wondering what his Da is up to, hoping he's still at Uncle Ted's where he said he'd be.

'We could go back to mine if ye like,' Una whispers when the others are preoccupied by a noise at the bar. Jude smiles but doesn't say anything, shrugs, pats down his navy jumper which is itching his skin. Her breath smells of the strawberry gum she's popping as she slides closer to him. The attention she's showing him is alarming. He's just so very unused to it.

He wonders why she's so interested in him when there are so many other lads with so much more to offer her than him. He cut his jaw shaving that very morning. Nicked it with his razor, placed toilet paper over the cut and watched in fascination as the paper turned from white to crimson and he had to replace it. He burnt the mince the previous week and spent twenty minutes scraping the bottom of the pan before giving up, admitting defeat. He keeps the teddy his Mammy gave him for his birthday when he was very little next to his pillow. It doesn't smell of her anymore, but he imagines it does.

He thinks these are things Una should know about him and then perhaps she'd stop wanting to fuck him.

There's suddenly swearing and shouting from the bar and Una tells Jude to 'ignore it, leave the silly arseholes to it,' but Jude strains his neck up, looks to see what's going on. Mutters 'shit' under his breath and leaves the table. Una follows. He's at the bar in minutes, apologising to the barman, tugging his Da's jumper, pulling him away. He nods when the barman asks him if it's his Da, says, 'Aye, so sorry for the bother, we're leaving. C'mon Da.'

His Da shakes his head, throws a punch wildly into mid-air at everybody and nobody, stumbles off his stool in an ungraceful clatter to the ground.

'Ach, Jude, get your auld man hame,' a man says, clapping Jude on the shoulder. 'Oi, Paddy, get yerself hame. Sleep it aff, ye mess.'

Jude nods, flushes red, takes his Da's weight on his weak, narrow shoulders, wraps his spare arm around his Da's waist.

'I'll help yi,' Una says, taking the other arm.

'Thanks Una,' Jude says hoarsely, struggling under his Da's superior weight. 'It's usually my best friend Kit who helps me out but he's away.'

'Away where?'

'Um, he's away on holiday. Been away for ages.'

'Ach. Ye must miss him, eh?'

'Mhm. Loads.'

He's embarrassed about the flat, runs around tidying up beer cans and empty pizza boxes that have appeared since this morning. Una shushes him, tells him it's fine, her Da's a drinker too, she doesn't care. Jude creaks the door open to his Da's bedroom, stands still until he hears his Da's snores filling the lonely space, then closes the door and joins Una in the living room. She's made him some tea.

'Shit,' he says, scratching his neck. 'We're out of milk. Sorry Una.'

'I take my tea without.' She's propping her elbows on her knees, leaning forward, says, 'So it's completely fine. Don't worry yourself.'

And Jude thinks that's actually really lucky, while also wondering if she's lying right to his face.

# We, Kit and Jude, invincible

We are children, Jude. We cycle for hours, doing everything and nothing. We build a den in your garden. Tie worn bedsheets around trees with thick rope your Da lends us from the harbour. Place your beloved tartan blanket over the top, a temporary sky for us to gaze up at in a satisfying array of woven welts engrained together. You take our sleeping bags from your garage, set them up inside, say, 'Look Kit, it's our new home,' and we lie on them, hands behind our heads, elbows touching, and look at those intricate designs.

Your Mammy blasts the radio from the house, leaves the door open with the light from your house illuminating our new home, lit up like it's something special. You smuggle out snacks when your Mammy's not looking. Biscuits coated in chocolate that melt onto our fingers as we eat them and so we have to lick the goodness off. Sweeties to make us high, coke to give us gas. We shove food into our open mouths until we're so full of sugar we're bursting for mischief. We never want the night to end.

We are spies. Our imagination knows no bounds. We are on a secret mission of the utmost importance, and we mustn't get caught. We push on oversized sunglasses which slip down our noses, dip our fingertips in the wet mud and pull them eagerly across our cheeks. We tear all the kitchen roll from the cardboard cylinders, discard it for your Mammy to find later and playfully berate us, cross yet loving with her cheeks red and her eyes twinkling because she really does love us, and we use them as binoculars, pressed to our eyes as we push our small bodies into the grass.

A creature appears, lurking in the shadows and we scream and run back to our new home, clinging to each other in giddy nervousness. We laugh at our stupidity when we realise it's only the neighbour's cat, Binks.

As the moon reflects off the tent and our happiness echoes around the neighbourhood, we creep out, feeling bold, and begin our secret mission again. Revelling in our silliness. We live in our dream together. Untouchable and invincible. Us. Jude and Kit.

We can do anything Jude MacAlennan, be anyone we want to be.

And we will, oh, we will.

# When you lose a sibling, you gain an unbreakable bond

Jude tells Mrs Lambert he has two sisters and three brothers. She tells him he's lying; he's an only child. His face burns scarlet. The others tease him, say his pants are on fire. He tells them they're wrong but they're laughing so loud and suddenly the laughter is all he can hear and it makes him want to scream and in his head he's just running and running until he's so exhausted he no longer hears their taunts.

'They're halfway babies,' he tells Kit, walking home, kicking the gravel under his feet. He's agitated. Has never told a lie in all his life, says, 'Mammy talks about them all the time so.'

'I believe ye. They're the babies who were almost here, but the world wasn't ready for them and so they didn't come in the end.'

Jude's eyes are suddenly wet. Blinks away the tears under his eyelashes, says very quietly, 'You've heard of them too?'

'I've a halfway sister. They called her Julie,' Kit says. 'She should be twelve. I think that's why I make my Da angry sometimes. Cause they got me instead, like. Mammy says I was a tricky baby and I just cried all the time, which surprises me because I'm delightful.' Kit winks at Jude, nudges him playfully in the ribs, before a more solemn expression falls over his face. 'I dunno if they'd even have me if they'd got to keep Julie. I dunno.'

Jude wants to hug him. To hold him. To finally have someone who understands. Sometimes he wants to scream so loudly until he's deaf. Sometimes he wishes he was halfway too because they get much more attention than him when his Mammy's sad, but he'd never say that out loud. Thinks that sounds too selfish, too cruel. Only thinks it in privacy.

When his Mammy tucks him in that night, she's in a good mood, and so he smiles, inhales the vanilla in her hair as it tickles his nose. Doesn't mention the others but he hopes they're safe. And then he thinks of Kit and the little purple bruises on his wrist, choking it like an ugly beaded bracelet.

Hopes he's safe too.

# Lonely only child

'When's the next baby then?' they ask, and they ask and even though ye smile and shrug and internally say, it's none of your fuckin' business, leave me be, still they ask. Big eyes. Round eyes. Nosey noses. Pushy. All wanting. All pressurin'. 'An only child is a lonely child.' 'Don't ye want a girl? Sure everyone wants a girl.' 'Don't wait too long. You're not getting any younger, Madeline.' You look at them with their ignorance, their tiny little brains and clueless minds, say, 'Sure, I'm only twenty-two. I've my whole life. All the time in the world. Besides, I want to enjoy Jude before I have another,' and they laugh right in your face as though *you're* the ignorant one.

And so the seed is planted. Once it's planted it grows. Ye can't unlearn it, or unpick it, throw it away, forget it. It's ingrained.

Ye try and try and Paddy's delighted, tells ye he loves all the fucking, gettin' lucky all the time, 'but sure, just don't set your heart on another. It might not happen. Just relax, Mads. Let's just enjoy Jude.' But still ye try.

And then ye want. Ye want want want. Christ ye really want. Ye want so much it's all ye can think about, ye can barely breathe the want is so powerful, all consuming.

And then you get. But then you lose. And then ye want. Get. Lose. Want. 'Ye can leave me, if ye like,' ye tell Paddy one night as he's cooking a meal. He likes cooking and your feckin useless. Ye wonder when he grew up, with his biceps and kind eyes and expanding brain. 'Christ, why would I want to do that? I'd never leave ye,' he says, and he looks so sincere and devastated that ye believe him. 'I love ye, Mads. I'm fuckin' mad about ye, always will be. We've got each other. We've got Jude. That's enough for me,' he says, wrapping his arms around your waist, strong arms, veiny arms, protective arms, man arms, his palms stroking your stomach. Your empty womb.

But all those faces in the shops keep expectin', those pushing prams on the cobbles remindin', ugly faces, slapable faces, sarky voices, all those questions still remain and they fill every space in your head until it's all ye can hear and it's killing ye, your undeniable failure to reproduce, and ye cannot say a bloody thing, until ye do, ye finally snap, and you're opening up in the corner shop to an eager audience, eyes open wide, leaning forward. And there's you, vulnerable little you, spilling how hard it's been, how many you've lost, hoping they'll understand and stop with the judgements, show ye mercy, pity, love. Leave ye the fuck alone. They shrug. 'Och, well, but at least you've got Jude. One is better than none,' and then they turn and leave.

Practically drooling they're so smug.

Ye cannot believe you've finally given them a piece of your broken heart. Sure, it's so beyond broken, it's hopeless trying to fix it at all.

# Something good in a day of bad

Jude's cycling, wheels kicking gravel underneath the tyres; the scenery is merging as though all the lines of oak, leaves and branches, are blurry and hazy. He's laughing, trying to catch Kit, but Kit's smaller, faster, and so he's ahead.

'We are going to miss it! C'mon!' Kit calls, looking over his shoulder, his youthful face filled with happiness.

Jude wills himself to keep moving, wishing his legs were as narrow and long as Kit's, that his stomach was flat and firm rather than feeling every bounce as he cycles. They come to a halt at the old railway line, discard their bikes. Kit puffs, bent over, gasping for air to fill his lungs once again. Jude places his hand on Kit's back, feels the rope of his spine against his palm, panting, sweating, thankful for the few moments of respite.

Kit peers into the distance and points, delirious with happiness as the train comes closer until their ears are filled with the hum of steel clattering against the tracks. Their senses are invaded with the smell and taste and noise as the impressive rhythm intensifies with the train passing, knocking them backwards onto their bottoms with its extreme force.

They lie on the grass for a moment, watching it become tiny and disappear, the track covered in a blanket of mist. Only, Jude focuses on Kit, who is sitting in awe, as though the passing train is the most impressive thing he's ever seen in his life, his skeletal face covered in freckles and bruises and muck.

'Something good in a day of bad,' Kit mutters to his chest.

'What's that?'

'Och, nothing really,' Kit waves his hands in the air dismissively. 'Ignore me. Anyway, I've got something for ye. A wee surprise.'

'For me?'

Kit tells him to close his eyes, says, 'do it Jude, please,' and so Jude nods, turns in the opposite direction. He's looking over his shoulder when Kit shouts, 'oi, no peeking,' and so Jude whips his head back, excitement bubbling in his stomach as he hears Kit rummaging in his backpack.

'Right, turn around then,' Kit says.

Jude does as he's told and looks down on the grass to see a sketchbook and some pencils, and a homemade card with a photograph of the pair stuck on the front.

'Like, I know it's not much but...'

'Oh Kit, wow.' Jude's voice is quiet as he leans down, picks up the card, examines the photo, runs his fingers over the sketchbook, the pencils, says, 'What's all of this for?'

'Nothing really. I just thought, like, I'd give you something nice.'

'Well, thanks so much. This is so thoughtful.'

'Yeah? Ach great!' Kit says, his face lighting up. 'I was so worried I'd, like, not bought the right pencils, or you'd hate the sketchbook, or you'd think the card was daft but...'

'No. It's all so perfect,' Jude says, swallowing, wondering how much Kit would've had to save up from his paper round to buy this for him.

Kit blushes, grins, looks down at the grass, says, 'cool,' then opens his mouth to say more but he doesn't. Keeps it shut.

They stay a while, Kit scribbling stories in his notebook, which he retrieves from his backpack, Jude sketching the outline of the railway, of the countryside, of Kit.

Kit. Kit. Kit.

That night, Jude runs his fingers over the scroll of words inside the card and smiles. He always loves everything Kit says, thinks even if Kit was to say something abhorrent, which he never would, Jude would still love his words. He brings the words up to his lips as though to kiss them, but shakes his head at himself, suddenly feeling foolish.

*Hi Jude, here's a wee treat for ye just cause. And you're the best drawer I know! Enjoy! Kit.*

When Jude falls asleep, he feels happy and content and warm, his mind an endless sea of possibilities.

# High on life or something stronger

There's music and grinding and dancing and you're eighteen and the bass moves into your soles through your legs to your chest and it's thudding and you're smiling wildly, widely, strangers all around but you don't care because tonight you are no longer Jude, you are bones and a body with a heart barely beating yet beating quicker than ever before and you are free and with freedom comes letting go of the ties that bind and pull you and you're not seeing anything now because there's just darkness with your eyes closed and your arms are in the air without a care and you're singing along with the music even though you don't know the lyrics because you are happy and free and you are not Jude, not him, anyone but him, and it feels like you're alive and dead equally and now there's a rumbling, grumbling, an eruption all down your shirt and it's gloopy and your insides are soup or maybe there's soup on the outside but it's hard to tell and your throat is raw and there's nothing more to come or maybe it's just the start of something much worse and then there's the cold cement and it's cracking your skull and you're falling, falling, everything's dark, and silent until it's not and there's a voice and they sound so kind and soft and caring and subtle you think you start crying and if you don't then you definitely want to if you are still capable of tears and then there's Una, or maybe it's Mammy, and she's tucking you up, keeping you warm, stroking your cheek with freezing hands which don't cool you down but soothe you, shushing you, promising you'll be okay, 'Jude, sleep it off, I'm here for yi,' and you know it's definitely not Mammy calming you because Mammy is dead, gone, cold in the soil and it's Una although you wish it was Kit, Kit, Kit and it feels like you're dying but it also feels like a new beginning too.

# You

It's gone noon and we're splashing in the muddy puddles, you and me, Jude; the water's right up to our knees. You're taller than me, broader, more muscles, more talented, more. You look at me with those brown eyes of yours and you grin, that delightful look of mischief, and then you grab my hand, and we sit down in the dirty water as it soaks the cotton to our skin and we're laughing until we can't breathe.

That morning in the caravan, you cut your finger on the knife slicing cheese for your cracker. Do you remember how it bled? Your Mammy put your finger between her lips and sucked out the soreness, kissed it, plastered it up, said, 'There Jude, it's all better now,' and you told her, 'Yeah, Mammy. It is.'

Your plaster's fallen off in the puddle now, sunk to the bottom with the stones and muck and dirt but you don't care, sure, you're having the time of your life.

Your Mammy strips us when we're back at the caravan, tells us off for taking in all the mess but she's not being serious; she's smiling. We stand there, bare shoulders touching, as she scrubs you down as you laugh and wriggle and complain it tickles. She hands me a towel, tells me to dry myself off too.

I see you looking at me.

I avoid your eyes because I'm embarrassed, Jude. Of the smallness of me compared to the greatness of you. You're almost a teenager now with that body, tanned and lean and brilliant. Your flat stomach, all those lines and definition leading down.

You're always more. More talented. More handsome. More loved.

And I'm always less.

The holiday with your parents ends the next day; feels like we've been here for minutes not days. I've never understood time, how it speeds up when you want it to slow down the most. I know my night will drag until morning when we can play together again, ride our bicycles to the railway line, mess around in the park; you can draw, I'll write. Our small things, our talents.

We sit together in the back of your Da's car. Your head is against the window; you're sleeping. You look so peaceful there, Jude, purring softly, all content and lovely, your lashes tickling those cheekbones which have come from nowhere and made you all grown-up. Your hand's just there, on the seat in between us, lying wide open.

I'm correct. The first night back home drags.

Everything's colder once you've experienced the warmth, you see.

You're standing outside the corner shop the next day, bicycle balancing against the wall, sunlight blinding you. You're holding your palm over your brow, smiling when you see me cycle up but your smile fades for a tiny moment as you look at my eyebrow, all black and blue like that, and then you smile again, pretending I'm normal.

You walk up to me and there's something inside me, like a butterfly, or a bursting burn, a volcano on the brink, fluttering, rumbling, erupting and you kiss me. You kiss me. Just above my brow, say very softly, 'There. It's all better now.'

And you're right. It is.

# Snow angels and real ones too

It's Christmas Day.

Jude's at the table, passing the sprouts to Mammy, who snatches the bowl from him, peers inside and makes a gagging noise, while Da carves the turkey and lights up a cigarette as a side dish. Mammy stands, helps Da take more of the food he's cooked through to the dining room. She's happy.

Jude's mouth is practically watering with the smell which seeps into the small dining room next to the kitchen and fills every corner of it, attaches to the very fabrics of his Christmas jumper with a cheerful fluffy penguin on the front, until he can no longer bear to wait and so he shoves a steaming roast tattie into his mouth which scalds his tongue, says, 'Ooo, ahhh,' and spits it right out.

Mammy claps him over the back of his head, says, 'Serves you right for being a wee piggie.'

Jude turns to her in protest, but she's smiling, shaking her head at him, hip jutted out at an angle, an expression of playfulness over her face and so he smiles right back.

Just then, the bell rings and Mammy tells him to get it. He rolls his eyes and Da tells him not to be so cheeky, to 'do as Mammy says', and so he pushes his chair out and runs to the door, wondering who could possibly be interrupting them on Christmas Day.

Kit's there, on the doorstep, in the T-shirt Jude gave him as a Christmas present. He's looking at the ground, kicking slush with the front of his shoes, and his forehead covered in ugly purple welts, spoiling him.

'Come in,' Jude says, softly, quietly, stepping aside.

Kit nods and enters, smiles, but doesn't meet his eye, only his armpit. They stand together for two or three minutes or longer, Kit shivering. Jude pulls his festive jumper over his head and hands it to Kit, who quickly puts it on.

'You can keep that. I've got loads and they've all got daft animals on them. Mammy thinks they're cute or something but, like, they're so silly. I dunno if I've ever seen a penguin smile.'

'Cool.'

Jude grabs Kit's freezing hand and pulls him towards the kitchen, 'You hungry?' Kit nods. 'Grand 'cause we haven't eaten a thing yet. I just tried to eat a feckin tattie and got told off. There's tons to go around. Da's a feeder, eh?'

Jude grabs some cutlery and sets a place at the table, pulls over an extra chair, takes a leftover cracker from the cardboard packet, says, 'Mammy, Da, Kit's going to join us for lunch.'

'So we see,' Da says. 'Sit down, Kit. I'll not be long, although I reckon I've burnt the whole feckin thing.'

And so they sit and eat and enjoy the turkey sodden in onion gravy with all the trimmings, pull crackers and tell jokes. Mammy and Da belt out Christmas songs, and then Mammy tells Da off for opening yet another can of beer and they're all laughing. Jude thinks to himself how lucky he is, to be here with his belly full, with Mammy in the best mood and Da smiling. Kit, safe and fed.

It's the small things.

'Oh, look, it's snowing,' Mammy says suddenly, pointing to the window, looking over their heads. Kit looks up and gasps, grabs Jude's hand and pulls him to the window, says, 'Oh wow, Jude, look! Christ, it's really falling! Woah! It's so magical!'

And then Mammy's wrapping them up in Jude's coats and hats and gloves and scarves, and they're in the garden, with the snow falling like flour, dancing off their rosy cheeks, and they're gathering whatever they can in their palms, squeezing their fists together to make small balls which disintegrate through their fingers, the air, as they launch them at each other.

And when they're exhausted, they sink down together to the grass, and Jude looks over at Kit, who's moving his arms and legs up and down, brittle like tiny bird bones, who says, 'Snow angels! Make one, Jude! Please!'

And so he does, because Kit's smiling so widely and he'd do anything for him.

Jude sees the snow angels that night as he looks out of his bedroom window, ready to draw the curtains, clean and warm and snug in his brand-new pyjamas, his toes newly cosy in his slippers as a smile spreads over his face like the sun rising.

Sees their hands and feet, all connected together.

# Losing your virginity, yourself and your preferences

Jude agrees to a date with Una not because he wants to, but because he's grateful for her. Appreciative of her lack of judgement over the mess he was in last month, seemingly uncaring that he's the son of notorious Paddy MacAlennan. The benefits of her being new to the town, he thinks.

He treats her to dinner.

It's a small restaurant, the kind where you're certain the entire place can hear your conversations if you speak at an average volume and so he practically whispers when they converse. She seems to like this, finds it endearing, romantic, somehow, to be whispering over the candlelight.

And then he goes home with her because she asks him if he'd like to, and he thinks, in that moment, he really might quite like that because he really is quite lonely. Finds it's nice to be reckless, to switch off, to be young and eighteen and free.

They're in her house and he's looking at all the candles on her mantelpiece, wondering why he didn't know she was such a fan.

'I get them every Christmas and birthday. I love them. Here, I'll light one.'

And then she's pouring him glass after glass of red wine, and maybe it's the alcohol, the smell of vanilla melting, or the warmth, the attention, but he finds himself relaxing and so when she asks if he'd like to go upstairs, he nods and follows her and when she takes off her clothes, he blinks heavily, barely breathing, but he doesn't dislike what he sees.

It's just different.

He slips his clothing off too, the buckle of his belt landing on the floor with a thud, and she says, 'Fuck, you're gorgeous, Jude,' and he says, 'Oh. Good. Thanks.'

Una presses her body against him, and her lips are on his. He stands, hands by his sides like they're welded there, unable to move, while her hands squeeze his cold arse. His body reacts underneath her touch, flinching, as though a current has been sent through it. 'Relax, babe,' she whispers, and he tries, rubs his hands up and down her back, in her hair, wonders if she likes it or if it just feels weird for her. It feels completely unnatural to him, to be here, touching her.

'C'mon,' she says, patting the bed.

He sits next to her. She's choking his cock with her hand, rapidly moving upwards, down, trying.

'Don't worry,' she says. 'You're probably just too drunk.'

'Mmm, maybe,' he mumbles, dark eyes staring at her, terrified, says, 'Sorry.'

And then his body lets him down.

Una's happy, and he's inside her, and the sound of their bare flesh slapping against each other echoes around the room, and he tries to make noises of pleasure because he does actually like Una as a person but not as a lover and as they're fucking he wants to claw out his own eyeballs, squeeze them beneath his magnificent strength and let them see all the particles of dust which collect on the carpet as his eyes roll away from his body and depart him.

Lucky fucking eyes.

And then it's all over, incredibly quickly. He's come within seconds, another betrayal of his body, fooling him into believing he enjoyed himself. She's lying by his side now, panting and he's staring up at the ceiling and he's hoping she liked it because although he didn't want to fuck her, not really, he wants to make her happy because she's so lovely and he realises in this moment he'd do anything to please her. And so

as she falls asleep, he remains very still, wondering
what it is about sex that people enjoy so much.
And he thinks maybe he's just no good at it.

# Mammy and the bin bags

There are two bin bags sitting by the back door, waiting to be taken out. They're full to the brim of rubbish, cardboard boxes, bottles, empty crisp packets, food waste; ready to burst. Jude's here now, chomping on his toast, sipping on his tea. I've burnt the toast. He doesn't complain, never does. Paddy wraps his arms around my waist and kisses my cheek, nuzzles his head into my neck. It's nice. I don't turn around. I'm watching the blackbirds swoop in and steal the bread I've thrown out for the sparrows. They just dive on down and take it.

Jude shouts that he's going to school now, Mammy, but I keep my back to him. Keep watching the garden, how the rain falls, unforgiving. 'Love you, Mammy,' he says, and his voice sounds so tiny it hurts. I swallow and nod. The door closes. He doesn't slam it like another boy might, in anger, in rage, or carelessly with a quickness to leave. He's thoughtful like that.

Christ, I wish I could be *more* for him.

Paddy asks if I'd like anything, some tea perhaps, or to go for a walk, hold hands like teenagers do. Says he'll cook something lovely for us to share later as a family. A family of three. Not four. Not more. Just three. Paddy, Jude and me.

The bin bags are starting to smell. The waste needs removing. Paddy goes to tie them up and I see it. The stick with the cruel, thin line and disappointment. 'You've got Jude, you're lucky. At least you have one,' they say, they always say. All these relentless years of sameness, my womb empty, lonely, without its most recent tenant after a misguided glimmer of hope. I nod. I can't say anything. What can I say? I want *more*?

And so Paddy, with his kind, brown eyes, says, 'I love you too, Madeline. We both do. I hope ye know that,' and he picks them up, the bin bags nearly giving way, the plastic stretching, threatening to spill over and erupt at any minute, but the plastic is strong, it holds on, keeps it together, its contents bubbling inside, close to the surface but they don't spill over, out, remain intact, inside, keeping it together. Barely.

And then Paddy tosses them in the outside bin. Just like that.

# Mammy stays in bed while the world ticks on without her

Mammy's in bed for a week. Jude makes her toast and tea, takes them to her, creaks her door open to the musty smell of body odour and damp, puts her treats on the bedside cabinet, hovers, just in case, but she doesn't say anything. She looks right through him. He wonders if he's dead, a ghost, invisible, but when he deliberately hits his forehead off the cold wall in the bathroom, he's reminded he's very much alive and it really fucking hurts.

'I miss Mammy,' he says to his Da when they're having dinner that night. Da couldn't be bothered to cook, which is really unlike him and so they've heated up a pizza with a side of potato smiley faces and he's treating them to a glass of coke, spiked his own with a dash of vodka.

Da doesn't answer him, just shoves slices of steaming pepperoni and stringy cheese in his mouth, gulps down his drink, burps, wipes his mouth with the back of his hand, makes a satisfied 'ahhh'.

'I miss Mammy,' Jude says again, quieter this time, then leaves the table and walks up the stairs, head down, dragging his legs. He stops outside Mammy's bedroom, just by the door, rests his head against it and listens to her snoring.

He undresses, pulls on a pair of pyjamas, slips into bed. He picks up the card from Kit and runs his fingers over the picture of them, says, 'Night then, Kit.'

And then he's in bed, trying to sleep but he's crying too much because suddenly the world seems lonely and cruel and he wants his Mammy to be happy again so he can be happy again and then his Da's there, in his bed, cuddling him, telling him, 'Shh, it's going to be alright son. She's just sad now but she'll get better. We just need to give her space and then love her more than ever when she's feeling like Mammy again.'

And Jude's nodding, holding onto his Da's strong arms, running his fingers over the protruding veins, hearing his kind heart thudding against his back, says, 'But Da, isn't there anyone who can help her feel better?'

And when his Da says, 'I dunno son, I dunno,' Jude thinks he'll never be happy again.

# It is darkness

The walls are bare. And the wallpaper is peeling. And the limp curtains are worn. And the sofa is worn too, stained, unfit for purpose.

The clouds fill the sky and dull the entire world, draining the colour. The sun has departed. Everything good is now gone.

Jude's standing in the doorway, head tilted curiously, examining the expression forever frozen on Mammy's face.

The room's busy. Strangers are talking loudly, movements are erratic, but Jude just stands for one or two minutes or longer, biting his nails, watching. He wants to be over there, holding Mammy's rough hand, begging God for a favour he cannot deliver, but he finds he cannot move.

And then Da's home, slamming the door behind him. He's staggering, falling into the walls of the narrow lobby. Laughs a hearty laugh with his affable face, glassy eyes and mouth wide, colossal body animated. He sees Jude, pulls him into a hug, says, 'What's all this feckin noise about then son? What's going on?'

And then he's in the living room and he's not laughing anymore.

# Small things

Jude's waiting for Kit, still clutching the landline in his hands. When Kit arrives, Jude's standing in the doorway, biting his nails, close to crying. Kit runs up the short path until he's at the front door.

'Help,' Jude whispers.

Kit nods, squeezes his shoulders, moves past him and goes into the living room. Jude follows him. His Da's there, soiled in his own excrement, slurring his words, cursing, drinking, turning to the side to vomit. Kit gulps.

'I told ye it was bad,' Jude says very quietly as Kit shakes his head.

'Nah. It's fine. Um. Right, can we get him up the stairs? Stick him in the bath or what?'

And so they help him stand, the weight of the world between the two teenagers, and Da's crying, saying, 'Sorry lads,' and they're holding him upwards, balancing, struggling, taking one step at a time, using all the energy they have to get him into the bathroom. Jude's gagging at the smell but Kit remains focused, unfazed.

'Grab some towels, Jude. Some clean clothes for him, pyjamas probably, if he wears them,' Kit says and then turns back to Da, holds his heavy head in between his hands, says, 'Yer a feckin idiot, Paddy MacAlennan, you know that? We all fucking miss her. C'mon then, let's get these clothes off ye.'

By the time Jude's returned with all the towels they own, Kit's cleaned Paddy up and is helping him into the bathtub where he's ran a bath, and then Paddy's sitting there, in amongst the bubbles, with his head tucked into his chest, sobbing into his knees.

'Um, I'll go downstairs and rinse those,' Kit says, picking up the discarded clothes.

'Oh, Da,' Jude says when Kit's gone. 'Oh, Da.'

'Jude, I'm… I'm sorry, I … I just miss her so much,' he says, and then Jude's in the bath too, his T-shirt floating upwards as the water fills it, holding his Da as he sobs, and then Jude's sobbing too, and he's saying, 'I know. It's okay, Da. I know. I know.'

He thanks Kit later, when his Da's all tucked up in bed, seemingly dreaming before the nightmares of reality catch up with him again and turn him incapable of functioning without Mammy. They're in the kitchen and Kit's finishing washing the dishes. He's cleaned the entire kitchen, scrubbed the surfaces until they glisten, thrown the empty food packets in the bin, transformed the room while Jude dressed his Da, put him to bed and changed into dry clothes himself. Kit pulls his hands through the last of the silky water and dries them on the dish towel, drops it on the kitchen counter.

'You don't need to thank me, Jude,' Kit tells him as he fills up the kettle. 'Sure, you'd do it for me so.'

'I'd do anything for you,' Jude whispers but it's lost under the buzzing and hissing of the kettle reaching its climax.

# Una Glover; friend, saint, mother (lover?)

Una helps him now that they're fucking. She buys them clothes – underwear, jeans, jumpers. She comes over most days clutching little Tupperware boxes, all labelled, with homecooked meals inside. Says, 'Ach, sure, I love cooking so it's no bother at all,' when Jude and Paddy try to thank her.

'There's a fine lass for ye,' his Da says when she's heating the mince in the kitchen, nudging Jude in his ribs. He tells his Da to 'shush will you' and sets the table while wondering if maybe Una should be his girlfriend after all.

He likes Una being here. Likes how she takes care of them as though they are hers to take care of. Finds he doesn't mind.

It's just the fucking he doesn't like.

The previous night when they finish, Jude cries in the bathroom. It's not because she's hurt or violated him in any way. It's more he feels guilty, because he can't feel the same way she feels about him intimately and he really wishes he could.

Tonight, they eat at the tiny circular table. Paddy had to sell Jude's childhood home years back and now they live in a flat by the harbour. The gulls used to keep Jude awake, forever pestering and probing just as he was on the cusp of sleep, but now he quite likes them. Finds he misses them if they have a night off.

'Cheers, Una,' his Da says, excusing himself from the table. 'That was a real treat. Yer a fine lass, so ye are. Maybe … maybe I can help ye one night. I used to cook up a mean roast, eh, Jude.'

Jude gulps and nods, gives his Da a small smile but Paddy doesn't catch it. He's staring at the refrigerator, eyes glassy, mind somewhere else completely. And then, just like that, he's shaking his head, sighing, back in the room. 'I'm gonna head to the local. Ach, Jude, don't look at me like that. I'll only be having a few. Sure, I'll be home by ten, I promise. Would yer auld man ever lie to ye?'

Jude watches him leave, the cool air of October seeping in as he closes the door.

'I'll do these dishes,' Una says, standing up, but Jude holds her wrist.

'Nah. Leave them. You're my friend, not my maid for feck's sake.'

And so they leave them, dirty, unclean, smelling, as Jude takes two beers from the fridge and hands one to her. They walk to the sofa. He's lost in his mind, when Una speaks. 'Do you miss them?'

'Who? My Mammy? Sure. She's been gone for so long …'

'And Kit, your best friend? Yi said he was on holiday?'

'Yeah, Christ, yeah. I miss him loads,' Jude says, gulping down the liquid.

'When's he coming home?'

Jude shrugs, takes a bigger gulp of his beer, says, 'Dunno, like. It was travelling, yeah, travelling that he went off to do and we just lost touch so. You know how it is.'

'That's a crying shame,' Una says as Jude nods and sighs. 'I could try and find him for yi, if yi want? Do a search on the computer? I can head to the library in the morning and see what I can find?'

Jude nods. 'Yeah? Yeah, okay then. Thanks, Una. That sounds really good actually.'

And he relaxes, sits back in his brand-new jumper and inhales it.

It smells new and fresh and hopeful.

# Some people shine brighter than others

They're sitting on the park bench, Jude and Kit, slugging vodka and coke from a plastic bottle, sharing a cigarette. There's Christmas music coming from the house across the road with the flashing lights, the smell of home cooking filling the streets.

'I fucking hate Christmas these days,' Kit says, his voice hoarse, husky, chilled by the cold. He takes an extremely long gulp, screws up his face as the alcohol burns his throat, says, 'Christ, that's strong, like. A Paddy special, no?'

Jude nods and pulls his coat closer to him, says, 'We could go back to mine if you like, but my Da's drinking and having a party and ...'

'Nah. Park's fine,' Kit says, his eye folded over, blackening, rubs it subconsciously, 'Da's, eh. Who'd have 'em?'

Jude laughs a little. Watches the snowflakes dance on the cement by their feet.

'C'mon. Let's make our own tradition then,' Kit says, tugging his hand. 'Push me on that swing, Jude. High as you can go so I'm feckin flying.'

'That swing's for toddlers!' Jude laughs but Kit's there, squeezing his narrow limbs into the cradle seat until he's in. Jude shakes his head in disbelief, pushes Kit as high as he'll go, the vodka swooshing from the bottle and hitting the wood chips below. Laughter echoing, bouncing from the metal slide to the seesaw and back again. Everyone and nobody can hear them.

'I'm gonna spew,' Kit says eventually, passing the bottle to Jude, who puts it on the ground. Wraps his arms around Kit's waist and pulls him upwards. Feels his ribs beneath his palm. The scent of his coconut shampoo floods his nostrils, his breath on his neck. They fall backwards, the back of Jude's head bouncing off the chips. Kit laughs, loudly, almost inhumanly. Jude remains very still beneath him and although Kit is light, extremely light, Jude feels momentarily suffocated with the proximity of Kit's body on top of his. And so he lies, looking up at his friend who is illuminated by the moon teasing them until Kit leans down, rubs his nose against Jude's, Eskimo kisses him, laughs slightly, says, 'Christ, Jude. What would I do without you, eh?'

Kit rests his forehead on Jude's for a few moments, but it feels like a lifetime to Jude. He closes his eyes, wondering what this could possibly mean, but then Kit's standing up, leaving his body suddenly lonelier than it was before, pulling Jude to his feet.

Jude's feeling shy, covering the shadow at his crotch with both hands but Kit doesn't notice.

Sure, Kit's just spinning in circles, his arms wide open, howling at the moon.

# Kit

There's a dream, Jude, one that I keep having. We're older, our bodies have matured, we are men, and we're smarter, I'm safer. We're living together, in a cottage which doesn't exist overlooking our railway line. It's lain empty forever because nobody wants to listen to the constant clanging steel, but we don't care. We love it.

You draw. I write. We ride until sweat trickles down our backs and we're both breathless, panting for air, discarding our bikes on the overgrown grass, completely spent. That's the dream. It's that simple. But it's brilliant. And it's ours.

I'm lying on the grass. My T-shirt is raised slightly with the breeze tickling my bare tummy, my palms are on my chest, feeling my bones underneath, my chest rising and falling. My eyes are closed when I feel your shadow fall over me. I don't want to leave the dream but it's you, Jude, and so I do.

'Sorry, did I wake you?' you say quietly, sitting beside me. I see you looking at my exposed stomach before you look away. You always look. I wonder if I disgust you: if you wish I was more too.

You've been further down the line, sketching a masterpiece, and I can see your drawings now, in your open pad. You're so talented, Jude. I hope you know that.

'Mhm, I think so,' I say, pulling myself up onto my elbows. Everything is an effort when it shouldn't be. I'm sixteen. I should be stronger, in the prime of my life, but I'm all bones and weak and tired.

'Sorry,' you say, and I shake my head, tell you it's fine, you've nothing to be sorry about. Not you. Never you. 'Christ, this nasty bug has really taken it out of you, Kit, eh?'

'Mhm. I'll be grand in a few days. Sure, I think that's the first bike race you've ever won. Gotta let ye win sometimes though.'

You smile briefly before frowning.

'You can go back to sleep if ye like Kit, sleep it off,' you say, your forehead crumpled with concern, those lovely eyes suddenly darker, your beautiful face, all contorted like that, worrying over little old unworthy me. 'I'm in no hurry to get home. Da's got Uncle Ted over and sure, they'll be trashing the new flat which is already a disaster. I'd like to draw some more anyway.'

'You can talk about it,' I tell you. 'I mean, missing your Mammy, your Da, if you're really sad … anything. I'm here, Jude. I'm always going to be here.'

I go to lift my hand to squeeze yours because it's just there, resting on your knee, open and inviting as always, your lovely hand with all those impressive veins running from it up your arm, carrying your blood, keeping you alive, but I don't.

Oh, Jude, it's not because I don't want to. I'm just too sleepy.

'I know,' you say, biting your lip. 'Thank you, Kit. You're the best,' and then you pause and look at me like I'm the only one who exists, and then you say, very softly, 'I lo-'

And I wish I knew what you said next Jude. I don't know.

I've fallen asleep.

# When Jude draws Kit, he almost forgets to breathe

They're in Jude's bedroom. The light is soft and there's music playing on the radio, but it's too low to tell what the song is. They're meant to be studying, but Kit has other ideas, more exciting ones that make Jude's stomach churn. Jude's got his notepad and he's sketching Kit, who's sitting, trying not to laugh, his jaw jutted out at an angle, his hoop earring catching the rays and half-blinding Jude.

'Have you always had that then?' Jude asks, pointing to Kit's neck.

Kit frowns and asks him what.

'That wee bump,' Jude says, sketching it.

Kit laughs a little, runs his finger up and down his neck. 'Nah, that's just my Adam's apple,' he says, pinching it between his thumb and forefinger. 'You'll get one yourself when puberty kicks in, my friend.'

Jude rolls his eyes, agitated. 'Not that, you muppet. I'm not feckin stupid. I've got one anyway, look,' he says, raising his chin and he's right. He does.

'I'm only messin.'

Jude puts down his pencil and crawls over to him, runs his finger over Kit's throat as Kit winces, says his fingers are feckin freezing, get off.

'Sorry,' Jude says. 'This right here, I mean. Have you always had that?'

Kit frowns, says, 'Um. Sure, I think that's just what my neck looks like. Why, is it weird or?'

Jude shakes his head and smiles, blushes. 'Nah. You're grand.'

You're perfect, is what he doesn't say, but oh how he wants to as Kit relaxes, turns his head to the side and stifles a laugh as he tries to remain serious.

When Kit's left, Jude keeps the windows closed. Keeps the smell of Kit inside with him. Thinks he'll never open the windows again.

# When Jude remembers, he instantly wishes he could forget

The positivity Jude feels is staggering. He's washing dishes in the kitchen, humming under his breath, his hands silky with the suds. He hears Una call his name from the living room and so he shouts that he'll just be a moment, he has one more mug to wash, but she shouts back, firmer this time. Tells him to come now.

And so he dries his hands on the kitchen towel with little doe-eyed puppies on it, grinning. It's one that Una's bought because she really likes dogs, and he finds he likes them too. Wonders if he will maybe buy one, one day, a dog for him and Una to look after, to love. He puts the towel on the unit and walks to the living room where he finds Una sitting on the sofa, brows furrowed, a piece of paper in between her palms.

He bites his lip and sways from side to side, the surge of familiar sickness rummaging in his stomach. It's a feeling he knows, although he cannot place why he knows it. She tells him to sit down and he does as he's told because he always does.

'Oh, Jude,' she says eventually, looking up at him.

He tastes metallic in his mouth now. He's been biting the flesh from the inside of his cheek, the sensation of blood and membrane crushed beneath his teeth.

'I think Kit is dead,' she says quietly.

He stares at her. Doesn't even blink. Then says, 'No. No, I don't think so.'

She nods, hands him the paper and there he is, filling the page with his wide smile and rolling brown hair to his shoulders. Kit Dornan. His Kit. Deceased. Two years ago. Aged sixteen.

'I'm so sorry, Jude.'

Jude stands very slowly. There is a feeling in his bones, heavy as cement, and so every movement must be carried out with extreme effort. He straightens out his jumper, although he realises it is not his jumper, not really. Gifted by Una. Like the T-shirt he wears underneath, luxurious against his newly lonely skin. Like the jeans which have moulded to his body and are now extremely comfortable, the shoes which still rub his little toe. Like the underwear, a size too large, but they cover his modesty and so he cannot complain.

Nothing is his and he feels it in that moment.

He nods, says, 'Oh. Right. I … I forgot. Thanks for letting me know, Una.'

'Jude …'

And then he walks out of the room, through the corridor to his bedroom, but now the cement in his bones has loosened, and he can feel his joints more supple as he moves. He pulls the jumper over his head, and then the T-shirt. Unfastens the shoes, and then the jeans, the underwear. A pile of fabric discarded on the floor. The socks are his, and so they remain. When he's wearing all he owns, shivering, he slides down the wall, doesn't feel the tearing of the little bumps of paint nicking his back as he does so. Doesn't feel anything.

Until he does.

And when he does, oh, how he weeps.

# Something like love

They're laughing, racing one another, over uneven ground, going off track now and again, and then back on the cycle path. Kit is winning, he's always quicker, fitter, free. They stop and park their bikes against the bark, panting, grinning from one to the other. Jude wipes his forehead with his hand. Kit wipes his forehead with the bottom of his T-shirt. Pulls it up. Jude blushes as he looks at the flatness of Kit's stomach, the way his pelvic bone juts out and leads down to his shorts. He'd like to touch him there. Just on his stomach. Just below his belly button. Just to know what it feels like.

'You want some water?' Kit asks, pulling a bottle from his backpack. Jude nods and catches it when Kit throws it to him. Gulps it down greedily. Laughs when Kit tells him, 'Hey! Leave some for me, aye?'

He sits next to Kit on the grass, passes him the bottle. Watches Kit take a few sips. The way his full lips curl around the tip of the bottle. Jude's wearing shorts and the grass unexpectedly tickles his bare thighs. He lets out an escaped little giggle and Kit turns to him, grins slightly, says, 'The grass tickled me there too,' and they both laugh.

They sit in silence for a few moments until Kit says, 'Ach fucking hell,' sighs, drops his head in his hands.

'Kit?'

Kit looks back up and squeezes his eyes together as though the world is suddenly too much for him. Jude thinks there's a new greyness to his skin. Thin lines constricting on his forehead. A redness in his eyes. Chapped lips. He wonders why he hasn't noticed this.

'Kit, what is it?'

Kit looks at him and for a split second, Jude wonders if this is the moment when he will finally kiss him. And so he sits, wets his lips, barely breathing.

But Kit doesn't kiss Jude.

Glancing in the other direction, Kit says, very quietly, 'I got my test results back, didn't I.'

Jude swallows. Nods, says, 'Oh.'

They say nothing, just listen to the sound of the birds chirping in the trees.

'It's fucking everywhere.'

The air is thin. Jude's head is spinning. A lump forms in his throat, wedged in, offers no respite from the pressing. He has so many words, so much he wants to say. Can only manage one syllable.

'Shit.'

'Yeah.'

Jude shuffles until he's beside him, rests his head on Kit's shoulder, closes his eyes. Finds Kit's hand and wraps his fingers in it, squeezes it. And so they sit until the rain starts to fall.

Thinks the world isn't fair.

Not really.

Not at all.

# Unfixable

There's a feeling inside Jude that's new. His heart is pounding. Ears throbbing. Hands shaking. And he's crying too, which irritates him because the sadness hasn't even hit him yet.

He's just fucking furious.

He takes out his sketch pad and scribbles repeatedly until the lead snaps and all that sits before him is an angry page. A flurry of anger and emotion. He rips the paper from the pad – suddenly as lethal and fragile as glass with his rage – into tiny shards that fall between his fingers as the tearing continues. Soon he's covered in paper and rage, and his face is wet with tears and snot. He doesn't know when his nose started to bleed and so when the paper starts to redden, he's alarmed. Thinks for a moment his rage is so extreme, he has somehow turned it red.

His Da's there, next to him, rubbing his shoulders, comforting him. Jude tells him to leave him alone, shouts, pushes him away, but his Da holds him until the tears stop. They sit like this for a long time, two bodies with two hearts and blood the same, holding the other.

'Kit is dying.'

His Da lets out a deep breath, runs his hand over Jude's head, through his hair, tugs it slightly, which makes Jude wince.

'Christ. I'm so sorry, Jude,' Paddy says, then after a while says, 'Christ. Not Kit.'

Jude looks at the bloody mess by his feet, paper that no longer looks like paper, old and withered and ruined. He wishes he could fix it, put the pieces back together somehow but of course, he cannot.

They're impossible to mend.

# The invitation

Jude first meets Kit when he's seven. He's in the classroom sitting by himself, sketching, in his own little world, chewing his bottom lip, ignoring the rest of the class as they play. He isn't aware of the new boy with brown hair, freckles and skinned knobbly knees standing by his desk, not even when he coughs a little, peers down at him.

'What ye drawing then?'

Jude continues to draw, doesn't look up. He's concentrating on getting the texture of the imaginary parrot just right. The boy taps the desk, goes, 'Ahem? Hiya? I asked what ye drawing?'

Jude looks up, startled, puts his pencil on the desk. 'Oh. I'm sorry. I didn't think you were speaking to me.'

The boy laughs slightly, says, 'Well, who else would I be speaking to, silly?'

Jude looks around, sees all the heads down, conversing, talking amongst themselves. Jude shrugs, blushes, says, 'I'm drawing pirates and their parrot and their ship. I've never seen a real-life pirate before, obviously, so I'm just making it up.'

'Cool. Can I have a look?'

'No way! It's crap just now. Maybe when it's better.'

Kit shrugs, says, 'Okay then, but I'm sure it's not.'

Jude smiles inwardly and looks back down, continuing to sketch. The new boy sways from one foot to the next, looks around again, then sighs, points to the spare seat next to Jude, says, 'Who sits there?'

'Nobody. Well, sometimes my school bag does if my shoes are muddy and I don't want my bag to be next to muddy shoes because my Mammy will get annoyed and have to scrub it clean. But nobody. Not really.'

'Fair enough. Can I sit next to ye?'

Jude frowns, says, 'Oh. Sure. If you like but I don't talk much, and I like to listen to the teacher so if you're going to talk all the time then I don't want you to sit next to me. I'll ask for you to be moved and I won't care.'

The boy laughs, his face bright, inviting, blue eyes dancing, sits down, says, 'I'm fine with all of that but I talk loads. Don't worry, I'll try and be quiet. I'm Kit Dornan by the way. I'm new.'

'I know. Jude MacAlennan.'

It's when they're in the playground, sharing a packet of crisps, blowing on each other's hands to keep warm in the cool November air which makes the hairs on Jude's arms stand to attention, that Jude cocks his head upwards, says, 'I'm actually looking for a best friend, you know, if you wanted to be mine.'

'Oh. Cool. I've never had one of those before,' Kit says, shrugs, smiles. 'Sure. Why not?'

And they are inseparable.

Until they're not.

# Life ticks on

Una brings Jude a mug of tea. He's sitting in his little flat, and his Da's showering, belting out a banger, and although it makes Jude happy to hear his Da happy, he still feels sad. He looks over at the mantelpiece, the photographs of his Mammy, the new photographs he's placed there of Kit which are old, a shrine to the people he loves, who he's lost.

He's sitting back down, listening to Una talk about her job, and he finds he smiles, he likes to listen to what she's saying. His Da's there, freshly shaved, clean, looking younger and happier, says he's got a date.

'Well, don't you look bloody handsome, Paddy.' Una grins as he gives a little twirl.

'Enjoy yourself, Da,' Jude says quietly. 'You deserve it.'

Paddy goes to open his mouth to say something but changes his mind. He just nods, gives a small smile. Pulls his arms through his coat and fastens the buttons. Jude thinks he does look really handsome; thinks he looks like Da again.

He watches his Da leave and then looks over at Una, who's now finished her tea and is spooning some yoghurt into her mouth, licking the metal, devouring every taste of strawberry infused with vanilla. He clears his throat.

'Should we, like, um, be boyfriend and girlfriend or what?' Jude says, blowing over the top of his mug. Una grins and his stomach flips. This is it, he thinks, this is it and his heart sinks. It's not because he doesn't like her, or doesn't think that she's wonderful, or that she's the one who has saved both himself and his Da and changed their lives for the better, because he really does, he really thinks the world of her, fuck, he may even love her a little, so it's not that at all.

'Um, nah,' she says as Jude raises his eyebrow. 'We probably shouldn't do that, like, but it's really sweet you've asked.'

'Oh,' he says; phew, he thinks. He wonders if he'll feel a new wave of sadness from her rejection of the relationship he doesn't want, but instead he only feels relief.

'But we could be good friends though, if you want,' Una says, squeezing his hand.

He thinks she's never looked more beautiful than she does in this moment, with her blue eyes dancing, her freckles joining like a satisfying puzzle, her red hair flowing, curled, lovely.

'Yeah? Oh, good. That sounds really good, Una.' He smiles, bites his lip, says, 'I'm looking for a new best friend actually. If you're up for the challenge.'

He swallows, closes his eyes, fights the tears, the lump, the familiar feeling of a hand in his gut, tugging, pulling, relentless. When he opens his eyes, she's looking at him the same way Kit used to, a look quite close to love, and he allows himself to believe everything is going to be alright.

It really might be.

You just never know.

# About the Author

Hannah is a writer and teacher from the North East of Scotland. Her Rom Com, *Life Lessons*, was longlisted in Helen Lederer's Comedy Women in Print Award 2021 in the unpublished category. She placed 2nd in the Writing East Midland's Aurora Prize in 2020 and won Cranked Anvil's first Flash Fiction competition. Her Novella-in-Flash, *Small Things*, was Highly Commended in the Bath Novella-in-Flash Award 2021.

She's been listed for the Brick Lane Short Story Prize, Retreat West's Short Story and Flash Fiction competitions, Flash 500, The Phare Magazine and Strands International Flash Fiction Competition. Her stories have been featured in *Ellipsis Zine, The Common Breath, The Phare, mac(ro)mic, Product* and others.

She's studying for her MFA in Creative Writing at the Manchester Writing School and is a selective Curtis Brown Creative alumni.

Hannah lives with her husband and son in Aberdeenshire, Scotland and tweets at @HannahWrites88.

# Acknowledgements

Thanks to my parents and Holly for nurturing this dream and supporting me unconditionally Thanks to all my family, in-laws and friends for always championing my writing.

Thanks to Jude Higgins and John at Ad Hoc Fiction for this opportunity and being a joy to work with. Thanks to Michelle Elvy for your generous comments and Highly Commending my novella in the Bath Novella-in-Flash awards and to Johanna Robinson for your thorough proofreading. Thanks to my talented sister-in-law, Emma Beaton-Donaldson, for designing the beautiful cover. Thanks to Nick Royle, Leonie Rowland, Rachel Fulton and Laura Besley for reading Small Things and offering your generous, lovely and thoughtful back cover quotes. I appreciate you all so much! Thanks to Emily Devane, for your feedback on, 'When gobshite Paddy drinks...' and Helen Rye for your feedback on 'Something like love' and 'Unfixable.'

Thanks to Chris Somos for your being the best critique partner and for your friendship. Thanks to Charlotte Chang, Jerry Donaldson, Jennifer McKay, Dawn-Louise Samuel, Nicola Anderson and Jenniffer Wilson for being my first readers. Thanks to my beloved beta readers Ruth Khan and Shelby Holt who have been there since the beginning of my writing journey and who have supported me every step of the way. Thanks to Leonie Rowland, for your endless support. Thanks to Curtis Brown Creative and the Manchester Writing School.

Thanks to these exceptionally talented writers who I am proud to call friends. Abhi Para, Alice Sutton, Barbara Whitfield, Dan Allen, Cathryn Campbell, Ed Crocker, Heidi Gallacher, Jen Hyatt, Julia Boggio, Lisa Nathan-Goucher, Paula Jones, Pip Swan, Samantha Quinn and Stacey Thomas. Forever grateful for you all- bring on the writing retreats!

Thanks to Leonie Rowland, Claire Smith and Becca Anderson for your endless support.

Thanks to Toby and Rory, for all things.